AT THE CROSSROADS

by Rachel Isadora

A Mulberry Paperback Book
NEW YORK

FOR JAMES

Printed in Hong Kong.   First Mulberry Edition, 1994.   10 9 8 7 6 5

Library of Congress Cataloging-in-Publication Data
Isadora, Rachel.   At the crossroads / by Rachel Isadora.   p.   cm.
Summary: South African children gather to welcome home their fathers who have been away for several months working in the mines.   ISBN 0-688-13103-4
[1. Fathers–Fiction.   2. Blacks–South Africa–Fiction.   3. South Africa–Fiction.]
I. Title.   PZ7.1763At 1994   [E]–dc20   93-11727   CIP   AC

Today our fathers are coming home!
For ten months they have been away
working in the mines.

It is early in the morning.
Our mother is waiting with
the others at the water tap.

When she brings the water home,
we take turns washing.

We eat quickly and leave for school.
On the way we meet our friends.
"Our fathers are coming home!" we shout.

We line up in front of the school and sing hymns. Thandeka plays the school drum. "Our fathers are coming home today," we sing.

After school we rush outside.
"Hurry!" Zola calls.
We are so excited, we start running.
We don't know exactly when our
fathers will come.
We go right to the crossroads.
We look down the road. It is empty.

Zola wants to play his guitar,
but he needs a piece of wire.
Sipho needs a stick with which
to play his drum.

We all go to help them look.
Nomsa has her can ready. All she
needs is pebbles to put in it.

Zola plays his guitar.
Sipho beats his drum.
Nomsa shakes her can in rhythm.

"Our fathers are coming home!
Our fathers are coming home!"
we sing over and over again.

People pass by and join us.
More friends come to wait
for their fathers.

Mr. Sisulu has closed his store.
He joins us and plays his drum.
Everyone sings and dances to our band.

The sun begins to go down. Lights flicker on in distant windows. People begin to go home. Mothers and fathers come for their children.

But we wait. We will not go home until our fathers come.

There are only six of us now:
my brother and sister and our friends.
We wait and wait.

Warm night winds blow.
The crossroads are very dark.
We see our mother coming.
She wants us to come home,
but she knows we will not.
She has brought us food.

Sometimes a car rushes by.
A goat crosses the road.
A truck stops and men jump out.
They are not our fathers.

Zolani is little and has fallen asleep.
We tell stories to keep awake.
It is almost dawn.

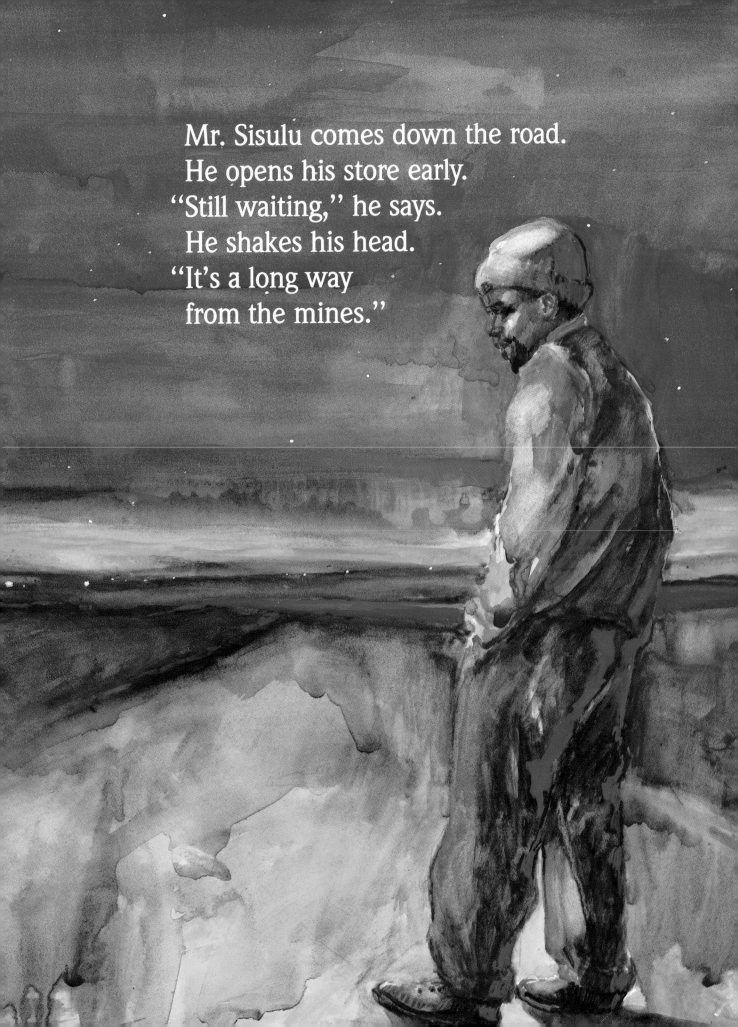

Mr. Sisulu comes down the road.
He opens his store early.
"Still waiting," he says.
He shakes his head.
"It's a long way
from the mines."

A rooster crows. Down the road we see two bright lights. We hear the rumble of a truck. We jump up. It stops at the crossroads.

Our fathers have come.
"Wake up, Zolani!"
"Our fathers are here!"
"Our fathers are here!"

We play music and sing.
We march home together.
"Our fathers are home!
Our fathers are home!"